TIME SPIES™

Where will they go next?

**The postcard predicts
a fee-fi-fo-FUN mission!**

Giant in the Garden

By Candice Ransom
Illustrated by Greg Call and Jim Bernardin

MIRRORSTONE

GIANT IN THE GARDEN

Cover art by Greg Call
Interior art by Greg Call and Jim Bernardin
First Printing: February 2007
Library of Congress Catalog Card Number: 2005935559

9 8 7 6 5 4 3 2

ISBN: 978-0-7869-4074-5
620-95613740-001-EN

U.S., CANADA,
ASIA, PACIFIC, & LATIN AMERICA
Wizards of the Coast, Inc.
P.O. Box 707
Renton, WA 98057-0707
+1-800-324-6496

EUROPEAN HEADQUARTERS
Hasbro UK Ltd
Caswell Way
Newport, Gwent NP9 0YH
Great Britain
Please keep this address for your records

Visit our website at **www.mirrorstonebooks.com**

To Connie,
my tale-swappin' friend

Contents

The Wonder Peas

Alex gazed out the window of the Keeping Room. Not even a leaf fluttered. It seemed as if the whole world had stopped.

"It's been *weeks* since our last adventure," he said.

"One week and two and a half days," Mattie corrected. She was nine and had the annoying habit of always being right.

Alex sighed, "This is the worst part—wait, wait, wait."

He remembered when they first moved to Gray Horse Inn, only a few weeks ago. He and Mattie had thought their lives were over. Back in Maryland, Alex was the goalie of his soccer team and had lots of friends. In the new place, there were no other kids around and absolutely nothing to do.

Then they discovered the secret in the third-floor tower room. The room had no door, but they found a way inside through a bookcase. But the real secret was hidden in an old desk: a brass spyglass that took them back in time!

Alex thought their first adventure was excellent. Mattie hadn't been crazy about going back to the Revolutionary War. But they met Thomas Jefferson and George Washington and, in a small way, helped win the Battle of Yorktown.

When they came home after the first trip, they realized that a Travel Guide had set up their adventure. The Travel Guide would only stay in the Jefferson Suite. For some reason, no one else ever booked the special room.

"Let's check the guest book," Mattie said. "Maybe somebody's in the Jefferson Suite."

Alex shook his head. "I looked already."

"Let's check anyway," his sister said. "Sometimes people call up at the last minute."

The kids ran into the hall, skidding on the braided rugs. At the same time, the front door opened. Alex narrowly missed hitting the middle-aged couple, who were entering with four leather suitcases.

"Kids," Mrs. Chapman said, coming in from the kitchen. "No sleigh-riding in the house."

She smiled at the guests. "You must be the Schmidts. Welcome to the Gray Horse Inn." Then she turned to the kids. "Why don't you two go outside while I get these guests settled."

"Sure, Mom," Alex sighed.

He and Mattie headed out the back door and they went out on the porch.

The porch overlooked the backyard, a jungle of gardens criss-crossed with flagstone paths. Roses, daisies, and other flowers crowded around the goldfish pond and tumbled over the marble birdbath. Birds nested in the tangled hedges. The sun appeared to teeter on the crest of Wildcat Mountain.

"—and they all lived happily every after," recited a small voice from behind an overgrown hedge.

"Sophie's got that dumb book again," Alex said.

"She must be telling stories to Ellsworth," Mattie added. "Anybody else would tell her it's 'happily ever,' not 'happily *every*.'"

Then a strange man's voice spoke, "I enjoyed that very much."

Alex exchanged a quizzical glance with Mattie. They ran around the hedge.

Sophie sat on the wrought-iron bench, her stuffed elephant next to her. An old book, *The Big Book of Fairy Tales*, lay open on her lap. A thin man was seated beside her. Alex had never seen anyone wearing a bowtie in the summer. The old man's snowy hair brushed his shirt collar. He had bushy eyebrows like white caterpillars.

Clearing his throat, Alex said, "Excuse me, sir. Are you one of our guests?"

The old man stood quickly on long, storklike legs. He was surprisingly nimble for his age.

5

"Yes," he replied. "My name is Wesley Taylor. I hope I haven't broken any rules. I wanted to see this magnificent old garden before I checked in."

"That's okay," said Mattie. "Is Sophie bothering you?"

"Oh, no. She's reading to me," Mr. Taylor said. "There is nothing more delightful than listening to fairy tales on a summer evening."

Alex thought Mr. Taylor made Sophie's

sissy stories sound like a Star Buster movie.

"I was going to tell another one," Sophie said.

Mr. Taylor dropped to his knees. Alex wondered if the old guy was sick. Should he call his parents?

But Mr. Taylor exclaimed, "Ahh!" He cupped his wrinkled hands around something in the grass.

"Did you find money? I lost a quarter out here last week." Alex knelt down but only saw a small white flower.

"*Jeffersonia diphylla*," Mr. Taylor murmured.

Alex shrugged. "Whatever." A flower wasn't anything to get excited over.

"Alex!" Sophie called. "Will you read my favorite story?"

Alex groaned, "Not 'Jack and the Beanstalk' again!" He had read her that story at least a hundred times. She never got tired of it. But *he* did.

"I'll read it myself." Sophie leafed through the book until she found the right page. Then she pretended to read.

"Once upon a time there was a boy named Jack. He gave the cow away for some magic beans. His mommy was mad and threw the beans out the window. And a great big beanstalk grew up!"

Mr. Taylor nodded. "My grandmother told me that story when I was growing up in the mountains. But her story was a little different."

"What do you mean?" Sophie asked.

"The story Grandma told me was called 'Jack and the Wonder Beans.' And other stories were about girls—"

Before he could say more, the back door opened and Mr. Chapman came out.

"Mr. Taylor!" he said. "I saw your car. Come meet the other guests."

"Certainly." Mr. Taylor nodded to Sophie. "Thank you for the stories. I'll see you all later." He went inside the house.

"What should we do now?" Mattie asked.

"There's nothing to do around here until we have an adventure." Alex kicked a large flat stone half-hidden in the long grass, stubbing his toe. "Ow! Darn these old weeds!"

Five shriveled green things lay on the rock's smooth gray surface. They looked like the peas he had once hidden behind the curtain in the dining room. He hated peas.

Sophie bent down and picked them up. "Magic beans! Just like in the story!"

"Oh, Sophie," said Alex. "They're just some dried-up peas. Throw them away."

"No!" Sophie clenched the peas in her

9

fist. "We have to plant them."

"Okay," he said, humoring her. "Where?"

She chose a spot by the tower. Alex poked five holes in the dirt and pushed the peas in.

"Satisfied?" he asked.

She nodded and then said, "Last one to the tower room is a rotten egg!" She dashed inside the house, clutching Ellsworth and her book.

"What is *with* that child tonight?" Mattie asked, as if Sophie were a tiny baby instead of a five-year-old.

Alex shrugged. "We'd better go after her. She shouldn't be in the tower room alone."

Alex took the stairs two by two. He paused by the round window on the second-floor landing. A half-moon shone in the star-filled sky. Travel Guides usually came on starry nights. But not tonight. He thudded up the steps to the third floor. The door to the Jefferson Suite stood open. But Alex turned toward the small bookcase lining a blank wall.

Sophie was moving the small stack of books from the bookcase. By the time Mattie caught up, Alex had pivoted the bookcase inward, revealing the passageway. They all got down on their hands and knees and crawled into the tower room. Mattie closed the secret door behind them.

The old, brass-knobbed desk was washed in starlight. Even when they weren't summoned by the Travel Guide to use the spyglass, the tower room was a magical place.

Sophie darted over to one of the long windows. "No beanstalk," she said, disappointed.

"Soph, you don't really think—" Alex began. Out of the corner of his eye, he saw the bookcase door widen slightly. "Matt! Somebody's coming in!"

An Extra Passenger

Green eyes peered around the bookcase. Then the rest of the black cat pushed his way into the room.

"Winchester!" Mattie scolded. "How did you open that door?"

"He figured out the secret," Alex said. "We'd better leave."

He scooped up the heavy cat as Sophie and Mattie filed through the passage. On the other side, Alex put Winchester down and closed the bookcase door firmly.

"Hello again," said a cheery voice coming up the stairs. It was Mr. Taylor, carrying a small duffel bag.

The elderly man stopped at the Jefferson Suite. Painted above the door were the words: "I *cannot live without books." Thomas Jefferson.*

"I cannot live without books either," said Mr. Taylor. "That's why I brought two." He held up two thick books.

"What are you doing?" Alex asked.

"Going to bed." With a wink, Mr. Taylor disappeared into the Jefferson Suite. The door closed behind him with a gentle click.

Alex stared at Mattie. Then they both spoke at the same time.

"Our new Travel Guide!"

The sound of pounding feet woke Alex. He cracked one eye to look at his bedside clock. Six forty-five.

Who was making noise this early? His folks would be downstairs, fixing breakfast, which was served at eight o'clock. None of the guests would be running in the hall. Then he remembered the Travel Guide. Maybe the running had something to do with Mr. Taylor.

Alex dressed quickly. He poked his head out the door in time to see Sophie hop down the stairs.

"Sophie!" he hissed. The family bedrooms were in a separate wing from the guest rooms, but the kids still had to be "reasonably" quiet in the mornings.

Sophie ignored him.

He took off after her. Alex knew she was up to something.

The door to Mattie's room swung inward. She stood there, dressed, but with her brown hair uncombed.

"What's going on?" she asked grumpily. Mattie was not at her best first thing in the morning. "Sounds like a herd of buffalo in here!"

"Sophie," Alex said. "She's on a mission of her own."

Mattie joined the chase. At the bottom of the stairs, they caught a glimpse of their little sister tearing out the front door. She swung Ellsworth by one red-velvet paw.

Low clouds threatened rain. But it was already getting hot.

"Soph!" Alex called. "Where are you going?"

Sophie raced around the side of the house and skipped through the dew-damp garden.

"Ick!" Mattie thrashed the air in front of her. "I just went through a spiderweb!"

Alex inspected his wet tennis shoes. Tiny dew-beaded webs like fairy trampolines were stretched here and there in the tall grass. Fairies! He was reading too many stories from Sophie's lame book.

Sophie stopped by the first-floor tower window. Squatting, she stared at the ground.

"Oh, no!" She sat back on her heels and scrubbed at her eyes with her fist. She was crying.

Alex reached his little sister in two long strides. "What is it?"

"Are you hurt?" Mattie asked.

"The seeds didn't grow a beanstalk!" Sophie wailed.

"Is that *all*?" said Mattie. "For Pete's sake, Soph, you scared us to death."

"Seeds take days and days to come up," Alex told Sophie.

"Not these!" she sobbed. "They're magic! They're supposed to grow a great big beanstalk."

"We planted pea seeds," Alex said. "Peas don't grow on stalks." He didn't *think* they did.

"It's almost time for breakfast, you guys," Mattie said. "Let's go!"

In the kitchen, Mr. Chapman was taking a pan out of the oven. Mrs. Chapman arranged muffins in a cloth-lined basket.

The kids went down the hall and waited next to the tall clock by the dining room, watching the minutes inch toward eight o'clock. The guests strolled in first, chatting about the good smells coming from the kitchen.

When Mr. Taylor passed, Alex gave a little wave. Mr. Taylor did not wave back. *Was this against Travel Guide rules?* Alex wondered.

Two couples sat at one end of the long table. The kids led Mr. Taylor to the other end of the table. A pitcher of orange juice and two pots of coffee stood in the center.

Winchester lay curled on his cushion in the corner of the room. Alex knew the big cat was only pretending to doze. He was really waiting for someone to drop a piece of bacon.

Alex sipped orange juice, studying Mr. Taylor over the rim of his glass. Today the elderly man wore a red bowtie and a pale blue suit. The last two Guides had worn clothes that indicated what they did. Mr. Jones, a Revolutionary War reenactor, looked splendid in his Continental Army uniform. Ms. Van Hoven wore the rugged boots and khaki pants of a paleontologist. Alex thought Mr. Taylor looked like a math teacher. Math teachers were okay in school, but would they make good

Travel Guides? He doubted it.

"Maybe he's not our Travel Guide, after all," he whispered to Mattie.

"He stayed in the Jefferson Suite," she whispered back. "He *has* to be."

Mrs. Chapman swept in with a steaming bread pudding. When she served Mr. Taylor, he said to her, "Did you know you have *Jeffersonia diphylla* in your garden?"

"What's that?" Alex asked. "Some sort of disease?"

"A plant," said know-it-all Mattie. "Remember? We saw it yesterday."

Mr. Taylor laughed, "That's the plant's Latin name. Its other name is twinleaf."

"Really?" said Mrs. Chapman. "What's so special about it?"

"Twinleaf is a rare mountain wildflower," the old man replied. "It was brought from the woods and grown in the flowerbeds at Monticello. A famous botanist named the plant in honor of Thomas Jefferson."

"How did it get in our yard?" asked Mrs. Chapman.

"It's possible Mr. Jefferson himself gave seeds to the first owner of this house." Mr. Taylor took a bite of the bread pudding.

"And it's still growing after all this time?" said Mrs. Chapman.

"Plants are tougher than you think," said Mr. Taylor. "Have you seen the roses around Monticello? Some of them date back to the fourteen hundreds."

"How do you know all this stuff?" Mattie asked, though Alex could tell she wasn't really interested.

Mrs. Chapman answered for him. "Because Mr. Taylor is a botanist, a plant scientist."

Alex's heart sank to the toes of his soggy sneakers. What kind of a mission would a *botanist* send them on? Looking for crummy old ferns?

"Oh." Mattie sounded as disappointed as Alex felt. "How come you're here?"

"I'm giving a lecture at Monticello for a garden club tour," Mr. Taylor said. "On peas. Did you know Thomas Jefferson grew fifteen kinds of peas?"

"I love peas," Sophie piped up. "I eat them with my knife! They roll into my mouth!"

"Yuck." Alex always pushed peas to one side of his plate. If their mission was about peas, it was going to be worst adventure ever.

Mr. Taylor gazed dreamily out the bay window and said, "Jefferson made a special study of peas. He grew the Hotspur pea, Leitch's pea, Forward pea, Green Admiral pea, Giant Sugar pea—"

"What about Green Giant peas?" Sophie giggled. "Those are my favorite!"

Alex looked at the stack of postcards on the sideboard. Travel Guides set missions into motion by writing on a postcard. The picture on the postcard showed the Gray Horse Inn until the Travel Guide wrote on it. Afterward the picture would change, giving the kids a hint about where they were going.

He got up, grabbed a postcard, and set it in front of Mr. Taylor. Might as well get this trip over with.

"Don't you want to send a postcard to someone?" he asked the botanist.

Mr. Taylor broke off his list of peas. "I suppose I should," he said vaguely.

Alex wondered if Mr. Taylor had enough training as a Travel Guide. He seemed new at the job.

As Mr. Taylor scribbled in the message space, Sophie said, "I planted some peas."

He peered at her over his glasses. "Did they come up yet?"

She shook her head.

"Give them a little time." Mr. Taylor checked his wristwatch. "Oh, dear. I'm late."

The old man dropped the postcard in the silver mail tray and then hurried upstairs to his room.

Usually Alex was eager to get rid of the other guests so they could peek at the postcard. Today he toyed with his food until the last person left the dining room.

Mattie fetched the postcard from the silver tray. When she turned the card over, her mouth formed an *o*.

"What?" Alex asked.

Wordlessly, she handed it to him.

The photograph of the Gray Horse Inn had been replaced with a scene of big green tree growing near a stone building. Alex flipped the card over. In the message blank, one word had been printed in large letters.

HELP!

"I don't get it," he said.

"Don't you see?" Mattie said. "It's *our* tower. Only ours doesn't have that tree."

Alex stared at her. "Our tower? We don't go on missions *here*. We go back in time, to someplace cool."

"We did go on a mission here once," Mattie reminded him. "On our very first trip."

Alex nodded. He hadn't forgotten seeing their house in 1781, when it was new, or nearly getting into a fight with Thomas Jefferson.

"That was different," he said. "We didn't have a mission then." He lowered his voice so Sophie wouldn't hear. "I don't think Mr. Taylor is really our Travel Guide. It's a mistake."

"No, it's not." Sophie had the keen hearing of a bat. "You'll see. Come on."

Mattie shrugged at Alex. "There's only one way to find out . . ."

With Sophie leading the way, the kids sprinted up the stairs to the third floor. Inside the Jefferson Suite the bed had been made but Mr. Taylor was nowhere in sight. Alex knelt and carefully pivoted the bookcase. He crawled through first, followed by Sophie, dragging Ellsworth and her fairy-tale book. Mattie closed the door behind them.

Alex ran to the desk and took out the box from the secret panel on the side. He opened the velvet-lined lid and lifted out a wood and brass spyglass. He felt both scared and excited as he grasped one end of the spyglass.

"Ready?" he asked Mattie.

She nodded and gripped the middle. "I don't like this part," she said, wincing.

"At least it's over quick," Alex said. He heard an odd *scritch-scritch* sound. Maybe their dad was cutting shrubbery in the backyard. "Ready, Soph?"

Sophie shifted her fairy-tale book under one arm.

"You can't take that book with you," Mattie said. "Ellsworth is enough."

"Okay." Sophie set the book on the floor.

Scritch-scritch.

What was *that sound*? Alex wondered.

In the next instant, three things happened at once. Sophie reached up to grab her end of the spyglass, the tower door squeaked open, and Winchester shot through.

"Winchester!" Alex cried. "No!"

The big cat rubbed against Sophie's legs. The spyglass felt warm under Alex's fingers. Their trip through time had already begun.

Into
the Clouds

Whoosh!

Alex dove into darkness feet-first. He could feel the spyglass in his left hand but nothing else as his body plunged into space. Rainbow lights sparkled and spiraled around him. The trip through time was never exactly the same. Today there seemed to be more green flashes among the red, blue, and purple glints.

He could not see Mattie or Sophie. It was as if they each took a different route, but wound up in the same place.

Thump.

His sneakers hit something solid but hollow-sounding. The darkness and sparks swirled away. A split-second later, he heard two more thuds. Mattie and Sophie appeared. Then came a lighter thud. Winchester dropped on all four paws. The cat looked so surprised that Alex nearly laughed.

"Where are we?" Mattie said, blinking. "What's Winchester doing here?"

"He came with us," said Alex. "I was afraid he wouldn't make it but he looks okay."

Sunshine poured through a long, narrow window on one side of an empty room. The light filtering through the window was a weird greenish color, like pond water. Alex guessed that the panes were made of green glass. The place seemed familiar.

"We're back in the tower room!" Mattie exclaimed.

Alex turned and saw the desk in its usual spot near the third window. Dust drifted over the wooden floorboards.

He smacked his forehead with his palm. "We didn't go anywhere! I bet our Travel Guide didn't say the spell right, or whatever it is they do."

"Yes, he did!" Sophie pointed to the strange window. "Look!"

The panes were clear glass, not green. Outside, an enormous, leafy tree towered upward, blocking the light and casting the greenish glow.

Mattie gawked. "Where did that come from?"

Alex stared at the trunk. It was smooth and green, not covered with bark. The tree wasn't a tree at all but a giant *plant* with heart-shaped leaves and curling tendrils. Countless vines were twined together to form a massive trunk.

"That's the biggest plant I've ever seen," he said.

"My magic peas!" Sophie danced around, jiggling Ellsworth. "They grew, just like Mr. Taylor said! We're in my story!"

"Wait a minute." Mattie put her hands on her hips in her bossy way. "We're supposed to go back in time, right? To a *different* place?" She looked at Alex, as if accusing him of messing up their trip.

"We did!" Sophie flung open the window. "This is our adventure!"

The vine, wide as their house, smelled like

31

a million lawns. Alex had never thought what *green* would smell like, but now he knew. The fragrance filled the tower room. A thick tendril slithered through the open window.

"It's *inviting* us," Mattie murmured.

Before anyone could stop him, Winchester hopped up on the windowsill and leaped on the waving tendril.

"Winchester!" Alex exclaimed. "Come back here!"

The cat skittered across the tendril and sharpened his claws on the trunk.

Alex leaned out the window. The tendril grazed his shoulder like a living creature.

"Winchester—no!" Mattie shouted.

Winking, Winchester jumped to the leaf above him. He scrabbled up on the leaf above *that*. Then the cat disappeared from view.

"What are we going to do?" Mattie cried.

"There's only one thing we can do," Alex said. "Go after him."

"What?"

"How else will we get our crazy cat?" Alex shot back.

He threw one leg over the windowsill and hitched himself up. The tendril arched like a bridge. Alex tested it with one foot. It seemed sturdy. Holding his arms out for balance, he walked carefully across the leafy branch, which felt rubbery but firm.

"It's okay," he said, hooking one arm around the trunk. "Soph, you're next."

"It's too dangerous," said Mattie, holding on to the neck of her little sister's shirt.

"No, it's not." Sophie jerked away from Mattie's grip and then tucked Ellsworth in her shirt. She scrambled up on the windowsill.

Alex stretched his free arm. "Come on,

Soph. I'll grab your hand."

"No!" Mattie shrieked. "She'll fall!"

Sophie touched the big leaves. "They're like elephants' ears," she said, walking over the tendril-bridge. Alex clutched her wrist and tugged her and Ellsworth to safety.

"Your turn," he called to Mattie.

Mattie shook her head. "I can't. You know I'm afraid of heights." She flashed a fake smile. "I'll just stay home. Send me a postcard."

"But this isn't home," Sophie told her. "It only *looks* like it. We're really back in the olden days."

What olden days? Alex wondered.

From the height of the great vine, he saw the goldfish pond and the roof of his father's shed in the backyard. But he didn't see any cars in the driveway. Their parents would never leave them alone. Where could they have gone?

Except for the empty driveway, the grounds and house looked the same as always. But the trees and grass and flowers seemed faded, like in an old photograph. Sophie was right—they were in a different time. Alex wished he knew *when*.

"Matt," he said. "We have to go after Winchester. And we have to stay together."

"No!" But Mattie didn't sound as determined. Alex knew she was weakening.

"Put one leg up on the windowsill," he said. "Now the other."

Mattie sat on the windowsill, her legs dangling outside. She glanced down and uttered a small scream.

"Don't look down! Look at me. Step on the vine. It won't break."

"If I fall, I'm going to kill you." But she followed Alex's instructions, wobbling across the

35

tendril-bridge. She clung to the trunk so tightly, her knuckles were white.

"I will *never* do that again," she said.

"We have to climb this vine," Alex said. "And find Winchester."

"Way up there?" Mattie gasped. "No, let's just go back home." With one hand she reached for the spyglass sticking out of Alex's back pocket.

"We can't," he said, moving away from her hand. "We still have to figure out our mission."

He noticed the multiple vines were twined loosely. He found a couple of handholds and began climbing.

"It's easy, guys," he said. "Use the spaces between the vines. Matt, you go first."

"Will you catch me?"

Reluctantly, Mattie put one foot between

the vines, then the other. Slowly, she worked her way up the trunk. Sophie went next and Alex brought up the rear. They climbed steadily, past the eaves of their roof, higher than the tallest trees, higher than Wildcat Mountain. Up and up they went.

As they climbed higher, they began to see flowers, huge blue, saucer-shaped blossoms filled with a sticky liquid. Alex wondered if the plants were poisonous. Sophie's shoe broke off a leaf that sailed down into one of the blue saucers. The petals snapped shut like a mousetrap. Then the flower burped!

"Don't touch *any*thing," Alex warned the others. "Just the vine."

"My legs are killing me," Mattie yelled down.

"Don't quit now," Alex yelled up to her. "It can't be much farther."

The higher they climbed, the bigger the trunk became. Where once the vine had been like one of the ancient redwood trees in California, it was now as big around as their house.

White ghostly clouds floated past Alex. The wisps became denser, like cotton candy. He couldn't see Sophie above him. He couldn't even see his own hands. His skin felt damp.

"Help!" Mattie sounded panicked. "All I see is white!"

"Keep climbing," Alex told her.

At last, they emerged, blinking at the blazing sun. Alex thought the sun seemed extra yellow, like the sun in one of Sophie's coloring books. The pea vine spread out into a garden. They were finally at the top, but the world they had entered wasn't soft and white. It was a dark, grim forest.

– 4 –

Into
the Woods

Tall trees with branches like witches' fingers blotted out the sky. Pale mushrooms pushed up between tree roots.

"What a creepy place," Mattie said in a low voice, as if the trees could hear.

"It's just like in my book!" Sophie clapped her hands.

"What do you mean?" Alex asked.

"The picture in my storybook. This is it!

We're in my favoritest fairy tale!"

Alex smacked his forehead. Jack and the Beanstalk! How did he miss the connection? Now he remembered an illustration in Sophie's fairy-tale book. It showed Jack clinging to the beanstalk and staring at a forest of tall trees and ferns like umbrellas. Just like this one.

"Sophie's right," he said. "I mean, we just climbed a giant pea vine right into the sky! We're in 'Jack and the Beanstalk.' "

"You mean, Jack and the Pea Vine," Mattie corrected. Even in a fairy tale, his sister had to be right. "I know what happens in that story," Mattie went on. "I am not going to fight some giant."

"We will if we have to—" Alex began.

He felt eyes drilling into him. Tipping his head back, he saw a brown-and-white owl crouched in a hole in the nearest tree. The owl stared at him with unblinking amber eyes.

"How come that owl is awake?" he asked, uneasily. "Don't they sleep in the daytime?"

"Maybe we woke him up," said Sophie.

The owl clicked its sharp beak and then swooshed down. The bird flew so close, they could feel the air from its kitelike wings. Talons flashed like scissors. Then the bird glided over the forest.

Mattie's voice trembled. "I don't like it here. Let's grab Winchester and go home."

"We can't," Alex said. The owl had scared him too, but he didn't say so. "We still have to figure out our mission."

"Our other missions were in real places, back in real times," said Mattie. "We helped paleontologists win the Bone Wars. We helped George Washington! What could we possibly do in Storybook Land?"

"We never know our missions right away," he reminded her. "The postcard gave us a clue, remember?"

Mattie nodded. "It said, 'help.' Maybe we sent it to ourselves. We need help to find that cat!"

"Where *is* Winchester?" Alex asked, glancing around.

"There." Sophie pointed into the heart of the forest.

The tip of Winchester's black tail flipped like a question mark before it vanished into a clump of ferns.

"That cat is more trouble," Mattie grumbled. "Maybe we should leave him here."

"No!" said Sophie. "He'd be lonely."

"Come on or we'll lose him." Alex parted a thicket of tough grass. "We'll never get through this stuff. I wish there was a path here."

Before the words had left his mouth, a stone-flagged path appeared at his feet. The path wandered into the woods.

"Wow!" said Mattie. "Ask for a million dollars!"

"I don't think the magic works that way." Alex stepped on the first stone. It was solid. "Okay, let's go. Winchester already has a head start."

With Alex in the lead, they hurried along the path. The deeper they walked into the forest, the closer the trees drew together. Soon the kids had to travel single file to keep branches from scratching their arms and faces.

And they were not alone. Eyes winked at them from knotholes in tree trunks. More eyes peered from beneath red-and-white-spotted toadstool caps. Every so often, an ear-splitting screech shook the treetops, sending a chill down Alex's spine.

The path became steeper. Behind him, Mattie panted, "I don't remember any mountains in that story."

Alex had been wondering the same thing. "These woods look kind of familiar," he said, "like Wildcat Mountain."

Mattie snorted, "We climbed a giant pea vine to the Blue Ridge Mountains? I don't think so."

Finally they reached the top of the mountain. The trees thinned, allowing them a sweeping view. Beyond, a meadow of purple and red flowers stretched from the bottom of the mountain to a round, emerald green lawn. In the middle of the green circle, a stone castle rose like a mirage. A sparkling moat surrounded it. Purple and red pennants rippled from its turrets. An iron bar latched the huge double doors. It was a picture-perfect castle, straight out of Sophie's fairy-tale book.

"Oh, boy!" Sophie cried. "I'm going to be a princess in that castle!" She started down the slope.

Alex pulled her back. "Not so fast, Princess Sophie." He spoke to Mattie, "Do you think our mission is in the castle?"

She shrugged. "It has to be. What else is around?"

At that moment, a figure stepped out from behind a nearby pine tree. Mattie muffled a scream.

Jackie

It was a girl around Mattie's age.

"What ails you?" the girl said to Mattie. "Ain't you ever seen a human bean before?" The girl slapped her knee, laughing. "Get it? Human bean!"

Sophie's face lit up. "Are you a princess?"

"Land's sakes, do I *look* like a princess?" The girl wiggled her bare toes. "Don't princesses have pretty slippers and crowns?"

"Who are you, then?" Alex asked.

"Name's Jacqueline. But you can call me Jackie."

"Do you live down there?" Mattie asked. She pointed to the castle down below.

"Me? Live in a castle-house?" Jackie said, "I live in a cabin with my poor mother."

"And your cow," Sophie stated. "The one you used to have."

Jackie stared at her in surprise. "How'd you know about Milky-white?"

Alex was beginning to understand. "Did you trade her for some bean—I mean, pea seeds?" he asked.

Her eyes narrowed. "You've been followin' me!" She folded her arms across her chest. "How come you're traipsin' around these woods?"

"We're looking for Winchester," Sophie

replied. "He's our cat. He has a little white spot on his chin but the rest of him is black. Have you seen him?"

Jackie shook her head. "No cats 'round here." She stared at them in their shorts and T-shirts. "You-all better skedaddle back where you came from. Or else."

"Or else what?" Alex asked. Was she trying to scare them away?

Before she could answer, Sophie pointed down the mountain slope. "Look!"

A black dot trotted across the drawbridge over the moat. They watched as it disappeared between the big double doors.

"That beastly animal," Mattie said. "Now we have to go all the way down there."

"Are you going to the castle?" Alex asked Jackie. He didn't want to just walk up to the front door and knock.

"None of your beeswax," Jackie said. "If I was you, I'd stay away from that castle-house. Ain't everybody as nice as me."

With that, she sprinted away, her bare heels flying. She ran down the hill, through the meadow and across the drawbridge over the moat.

The Giant and His Wife

"How rude!" Mattie said. "That girl didn't even say goodbye."

"Don't you know who she is?" asked Alex.

"Sure, her name's Jackie—"

Alex waved his arms with excitement. "She's *Jack* in 'Jack in the Beanstalk.' Only she's a girl. Get it?"

Mattie's mouth dropped open. "She climbed our vine! She's—"

"—headed for big trouble," Alex finished for her. "Remember the story?"

"I tried to *tell* you," Sophie said.

"Yes, you did, Soph," said Alex. "Now we know our mission. To save Jackie from the giant!"

"But who's going to save *us*?" Mattie argued.

"We don't need saving. We know the story, but Jackie doesn't. The giant doesn't know it either." Alex crossed his fingers behind his back. He *hoped* the giant didn't know the story.

"But in the story, Jack gets what he wants," said Mattie. "Jackie doesn't need our help."

Alex thought a moment. "But things are changed. Like, we climbed a pea vine instead of a beanstalk. And Jack is a girl. The ending might be different too."

"Let's go across the river to the castle!" Sophie shouted.

"It's a moat," Alex told her. "And don't yell. We don't know who—or what—might be listening."

He ran the rest of the way, ahead of Mattie and Sophie. He couldn't wait to get inside the castle. Maybe he'd find a suit of armor to wear. At the drawbridge, they crept over the wide wooden planks, up to the arched double doors. The black iron bar had been pulled back from the iron latch and the right-hand door stood open a foot or so.

"Squeeze through," Alex whispered. "Matt, you first."

She slipped through the gap, waggling her fingers that it was safe. Alex followed Sophie inside.

"What a dump," Mattie remarked, squinting in the dim light. "I thought a castle would have fancy chandeliers and velvet rugs."

"Maybe the giant isn't into decorating," Alex said. His stomach fizzed with nervousness. Where *was* the giant?

They pattered down a huge stone corridor lit by torches in iron brackets. The air was cool and damp. Along the way, they saw piles of debris.

"Somebody is a slob," said Mattie in disgust. "Look at all these white sticks."

Alex gulped. "Matt, those are bones."

Arm bones, leg bones, and backbones littered the floor.

"Whose were they?" Mattie whispered.

"I don't know," said Alex. "But if anybody asks you to stay for dinner, say no!"

Mattie pointed to a figure creeping down the hall. "Look, there's Jackie."

Jackie zipped into a room off the corridor.

"After her!" Alex ordered.

The kids ran to the room Jackie had disappeared into. They halted just inside the doorway. It was a kitchen, with an old-fashioned stove the size of a van. The cupboard could be used as a climbing wall and the brick oven could hide fifty cats. The rest of the furnishings consisted of a plain wooden table and two straight-back chairs.

But Alex wasn't interested in the furniture. He stared at a gigantic woman shaking pepper into a pot on the stove. She wore a long apron and a patched dress like Jackie's. A white frilled cap covered her wiry reddish hair.

"The giant's wife!" Sophie sang happily.

"Shhh!" Mattie said, and Alex herded them behind a chair leg.

But the giant's wife didn't pay them any attention. She stared at Jackie, who had scuttled out from underneath the cupboard.

"Who are you?" the woman demanded, grabbing a soup ladle. Alex wondered if she was going to bash Jackie with it.

"I'm Jackie." Jackie didn't seem worried that she was speaking to a giant.

The woman shook the ladle at Jackie. "Don't you know my husband hates all children?"

"How could I know that?" Jackie tossed her pigtails. "I just got here."

Alex admired her bravery. But he knew from the story that Jack was *too* brave and took terrible risks. He was afraid Jackie would do the same.

"My husband can smell a child a mile away." The giant's wife froze. "Here he comes now! Quick, hide!"

She yanked the oven door open, picked Jackie up as if she were a doll, threw her inside, and slammed the door shut.

Thrum! Thrum!

The floor quaked as heavy footsteps drew closer. Alex, Mattie, and Sophie huddled together behind the chair leg. The room darkened. A massive man filled the doorway. He was even taller than his wife.

"WIFE, WHERE'S MY BREAKFAST!" he thundered.

The giant stomped in, making the dishes rattle in the cupboard, and sat down.

"Right here!" his wife barked back. She slammed a bowl the size of a bathtub in front of him.

"ABOUT TIME." The giant sneezed, picked up his spoon, and began eating.

From behind the chair leg, Alex watched the giant slobber oatmeal all over the place. A gob fell on the floor right next to Alex. If it had hit him, he would have been slimed.

Sophie wrinkled her nose. "He needs a bib."

At last the oatmeal blizzard stopped and the giant pushed the bowl away.

"WIFE! BRING ME MY GOLD!" he demanded.

"How rude," Mattie said. "Hasn't he ever heard the word *please*?"

His wife brought over an enormous burlap sack and plunked it on the table. "You messed up my nice clean floor," she muttered, storming out of the room.

"WHO CARES!"

The giant opened the sack. Gold coins spilled out across the table in a glittering river. The coins glinted in the torchlight.

Alex gasped. "He must have a million dollars!"

"A trillion-zillion," Sophie put in.

"Too bad he doesn't drop one of those," Mattie whispered. "We could be rich the rest of our lives."

The giant began sorting the coins. "ONE, TWO, THREE—" He sneezed again.

He reached into his shirt pocket and pulled out a handkerchief the size of a bedsheet. He wiped his nose, snorted, and then went back to counting. "THREE . . . THREE."

"He doesn't know what comes after

three!" Mattie said.

"No, he keeps losing his place," said Alex, who had a better view of the tabletop.

"He has to start over."

"ONE, TWO . . ." The giant bent over his task, concentrating.

A small movement caught Alex's eye. The oven door creaked open. Jackie's head popped out. Her eyes went round at the sight of the gold.

"Uh-oh," Alex said. "She's going after the gold, just like in the story!"

Jackie edged along the brick oven ledge, heading for the table. Her mouth was set in a determined line.

"We can't let her try!" Mattie said. "He'll squash her!"

"We have to get the gold ourselves," said Alex.

He studied the giant's leg next to him. He wore trousers of a rough, coarse-woven fabric. The pants were loose, falling in valleys and folds down to the giant's muddy boot. Alex thought of a plan.

He whispered to the others, "Here's what we're going to do . . ."

By now Jackie was poised to jump over the giant's shoulder and onto the table. Before she leaped, Alex sprang out from behind the chair.

"Nyah! Nyah! Nyah!" he yelled at the top of his lungs.

At the same instant, Mattie and Sophie scampered up the giant's leg, using the fabric folds as steps. By the time they reached the table, the giant was on his feet, heading for Alex.

"IS THAT A CHILD?" he bellowed. "HOW DARE YOU COME IN MY CASTLE!"

"Can't catch me!" Alex yelled, skipping around to taunt the giant.

Mattie and Sophie pushed the coins back in the bag and dragged it to the edge of the table. Jackie hopped down and helped them. They slid down the table leg, hefting the bag of gold between them.

"This way!" Alex yelled, running to the door.

The girls hobbled out of the kitchen and down the hall, dragging the heavy sack. Alex picked up one end so they could move faster.

"BRING BACK MY GOLD!" the giant roared, stamping after them.

The kids stayed close to the wall away from the giant's crushing boots. They tripped over the bones, but kept going. At last they saw the door and wiggled through the opening. The bag of gold got stuck, but Alex kicked it through. Outside, they pelted across the drawbridge. Then Alex stopped, still carrying the sack.

"Hand it over," Jackie demanded. "I mean to have that money-bag."

Alex thrust it at her. "Here. Go home to your mother."

"What about you-all?" Jackie asked, her arms full of gold.

"We can't leave yet," said Mattie. "We still have to find our cat."

"Suit yourself," Jackie said, and dashed through the meadow. Even weighed down with the sack, she ran like lightning.

Thrum! *Thrum!* The boards of the draw-bridge groaned. A huge shadow fell over the kids.

The Tiny
Little Chicken

FEE, FAW, FUMM," a voice thundered. "I SMELL THE BLOOD OF AN ENGLISH-MUM. BEIN' HE DEAD OR BEIN' HE ALIVE, I'LL GRIND HIS BONES TO EAT WITH MY PONES."

The giant lurched toward the kids and tried to catch all three of them at once.

"Split up!" Alex yelled.

He and Sophie each ducked under one of the giant's arms. Mattie scooted around him to the drawbridge.

The giant snatched empty air, which made him angrier. "I'LL GET YOU!"

He squatted down, blocking the end of the drawbridge like a bus.

"Go back inside the castle!" Mattie cried from behind the giant's back. "It's our only chance!"

Alex and Sophie skittered beneath the giant and into the castle. Mattie tried to push the door closed.

By now the giant had lumbered to his feet. He flung the doors open, took two steps inside, and then sneezed.

"AAA-CHOO!"

His sneeze blew the kids' hair straight back and zapped most of the torches lining the corridor. In the dark, Alex stumbled over the bones. At least the giant could no longer see the three of them. Then he heard a loud sniffing sound.

Mattie inhaled sharply. "He can *smell* us," she whispered. "Just like in the story."

The giant sneezed again.

"He can't smell us!" Alex said. "Not with that giant-size cold! We're safe, at least for now."

They scurried down the hall past the kitchen. The corridor branched into two smaller hallways. The kids veered right, down a hall lit with sputtering torches. Ahead they saw a furry black shape lurking by an arched doorway.

"Winchester!" Sophie exclaimed. "Here, kitty, kitty!"

Winchester turned to regard them with eyes that said, *Are you talking to me*? Then he slipped into the room.

"That cat is sure having fun," Mattie said, as they hurried to follow him.

The room's furnishings were sparse—a table, a chair, and a tall cabinet topped with a small brass cage. Columns carved with leering faces soared to a golden ceiling. The golden ceiling washed the room with a soft, yellow glow. The giant thudded in. The kids nipped behind a column.

"I KNOW YOU'RE IN HERE!" he rumbled. "I'LL HAVE YOU FOR MY SUPPER!"

Just then the giant's wife came in. "Are you still fussing about those children? They're long gone."

"NO, THEY AREN'T! THEY'RE IN HERE SOMEWHERE. I SAW THEM."

"That's just your cold," his wife said. "Your eyes are watery and you're seeing things."

"I AM NOT SEEING THINGS!"

"I'm making a nice stew for your supper. Four hogs, three sheep, and five dozen quail.

That should fill up even your stomach." Then her tone changed. "Look at this mud on the floor! How many times have I told you to wipe your boots?"

Alex peeked around the column. He could see the cage on top of the cabinet. Something moved inside. And something moved *outside* as well. A black paw slithered between the wires.

Alex elbowed Mattie. "Winchester strikes again," he whispered. "We have to catch him before the giant does."

"How?" asked Mattie. "We'll never get up there."

"Look," said Sophie.

A pig-tailed figure appeared in the doorway. Jackie! She raced across the room and slid behind the column with the kids.

"Hi-dy," she said, grinning. She wore a knife stuck in her belt.

"What are you doing here?" Alex whispered.

"I dropped the money-bag down the pea vine and came back," she said. "Wondered what else the man-giant had."

"Did you steal that knife from the giant?" asked Alex.

She shook her head. "Traded it."

Now the giant sat down with a grunt. "BRING ME MY HEN," he ordered his wife.

"You're as lazy as a leaf," she griped. "The hen isn't two feet from you."

She fetched the brass cage and plunked it on the table. Then she stalked out of the room, muttering to herself about good-for-nothing man-giants.

The kids crept out from behind the column. Winchester was gone.

The giant's hammy fingers fumbled with the latch on the cage. Finally he got it open. A tiny, black hen stepped out daintily and strutted around the table. The hen was half the size of a regular chicken and smaller than the giant's pinky fingernail. The giant leaned down, his bulbous nose level with the tabletop. His breath tumbled the little bird backward.

Sophie was delighted. "Look at the tiny little chicken! Isn't it cute?"

"It's a banty hen," Jackie said. "The teeniest fowl in the barnyard. But they're feisty little critters."

The hen glared at the giant with beady eyes. Then she pecked his nose.

"OUCH!" The giant rubbed his nose. "LAY!"

Alex knew what was coming next. In Sophie's book, it was a normal-size red hen. But he was sure this little black hen had the same power. He wondered how to keep Jackie from acting crazy again.

The hen settled her feathers and wiggled her rump. Then a golden egg rolled across the table.

Jackie gasped, "It's pure gold!"

"LAY!" the giant commanded. The hen laid another golden egg. "LAY! LAY! LAY!" the giant repeated. Soon the hen roosted on top of a hill of golden eggs.

Even though Alex had seen the illustration in Sophie's book, watching a chicken lay golden eggs in real life was amazing. The eggs gleamed, smooth and perfect.

"I mean to have that banty hen," Jackie said. "Them golden eggs will feed me and Mama the rest of our born days."

"You can't eat gold eggs," Mattie pointed out.

"No, but we can sell 'em and have ham-meat and stack-cake three times a day."

Jackie shifted from foot to foot, ready to run.

Alex grabbed her arm. "The giant's already mad about the gold you stole. He'll squish you for sure."

Jackie jerked away. "You-all stay back. This is a job for the fearless."

"We're just as brave as you are!" Mattie said.

Alex thought a moment. If only they had a weapon of some sort. Jackie's knife wouldn't cause much damage. His foot kicked something and sent it spinning: a clump of mud the giant had tracked in. Ammo!

"We'll distract him again," he said. "When I give the signal, fire these mud balls. Matt, you climb up and grab the hen."

"No, me!" Sophie said. "Let me get the tiny little chicken!"

Before Alex could stop her, Sophie bolted for the giant's boot. Alex, Mattie, and Jackie flew out from behind the column. Alex picked up a dirt clod and hurled it. The hard lump of dirt clipped the giant's ear.

"OW!" The giant cupped his ear.

Mattie and Jackie began bombarding the giant too, until he ducked under the hailstorm of mud clods.

Sophie shinnied up the giant's boot and pulled herself up his pant leg. By the time she reached the table, the giant had covered his head with his arms. He didn't see her scamper across the table and seize the little black hen.

Alex saw her jump down and run out the door. Throwing a last fistful of mud, he hustled out of the kitchen too. Mattie and Jackie were on his heels.

"BRING BACK MY HEN!" the giant exploded. Heaving over the table, he stomped after them.

The kids flew down the hallway and turned down the main corridor.

Alex took the chicken from Sophie.

The hen squawked, *Buck! Buck! Squa-awk!*

"Be quiet, you feathered tattletale," Alex told it.

The giant heard his hen and boomed, "STOP, YOU PINT-SIZE THIEVES!"

The door loomed ahead of them. The kids shot through and across the drawbridge.

Thrum! Thrum! Thrum!

The drawbridge shivered. Alex was afraid the boards would splinter under the giant's weight.

They dashed through the meadow and up

the mountain. Alex had a stitch in his side, but they couldn't slow down. Though they were quicker, the giant took larger steps and covered more ground. Their only chance was to lose him in the forest.

"WHERE ARE YOU LITTLE VARMINTS?"

A tree crashed. Then another. Alex glanced back to see the giant rip an oak out of the earth by its roots, and then toss the tree aside like a twig.

"He's tearing up the forest!" he exclaimed. "We won't have anyplace to hide!"

Suddenly the crashing stopped. Alex wondered if the giant had given up and gone back to the castle. The kids stopped to catch their breath.

"Give me the banty hen," said Jackie.

Alex was only too glad to hand it over. "Go home," he told her. "And *don't* come back!"

"Thanks!" Flashing her grin, Jackie tore into the forest.

"Do you think she'll listen this time?" Mattie asked Alex. "She's stubborn."

"If she were smart, she'd stay away."

"But that's not how the story goes," Mattie said with a sigh. "Alex, if Jackie is going to get all the giant's treasures anyway, why does she need us?"

"Because this isn't *exactly* like the story we know," he said. "Something could still go wrong. She only has two of the treasures."

"The treasures have been the same, at least," said Mattie. "The bag of gold, the hen that laid the golden eggs—"

"One more treasure to go," Alex said.

But Mattie's gaze was fixed on something over his shoulder.

Alex felt a blast of hot wind on the back

of his neck. No, not wind. Stinky breath. He tensed, expecting boa-constrictor fingers to squeeze his middle.

"LOOKEE WHAT I FOUND."

Alex turned around. Spitting and swinging, Winchester dangled between the giant's thumb and forefinger.

— 8 —

The Magic Quilt

Winchester looked like a mouse in the giant's big fingers. The giant sneered, showing teeth like rusted car doors. Then he dropped Winchester in his left shirt pocket and swiped at the kids.

"Make a break for it!" Alex shouted. He pushed Sophie and Mattie ahead of him. They took off, dodging the giant's scoop-shovel hand.

"But he's got Winchester!" Sophie wailed. "We have to save him!"

"Save yourself first," Alex said. He fled toward the castle.

"I'LL GET YOU THIS TIME!"

The giant tramped through the woods. Instead of vaulting the fallen trees, the kids crawled underneath. The giant tried to follow, but his big boots hooked on the first log and he toppled like a tree himself.

WHOMP!

The ground trembled like a major earthquake. The giant sprawled in a heap of arms and legs, moaning. He rolled on his side and lay still.

"Winchester!" Sophie cried.

"He fell on his other side, so Winchester's okay," Mattie told her. "But when the giant wakes up, he's going to have a supersize headache."

"Alex," Sophie begged. "Get Winchester out of the giant's pocket!"

"He might come to," Alex told her. Sophie started to wail. "Shhh! The giant will go back to the castle. We'll be there first. And I'll figure out a plan." I *hope*, he thought.

They rambled through the forest, going first in one direction, then another. Nothing seemed familiar.

"This isn't the way to the castle," Mattie declared. "We're lost."

"In fairy tales, a talking frog or something helps people," said Alex. "Where is a talking frog when you need one?"

"Here," a voice croaked.

Mattie stared at Alex. "Are you *sure* we can't ask for a million dollars?"

Someone stepped from behind a tree. Not a frog, but an old witch woman with a beaky nose. Her amber eyes peered at them from the hood of her brown cloak.

"Stay back!" Alex warned. "Who are you?"

"Don't be a fool," the witch said. "I'm here to help you."

"How do we know we can trust you?" Mattie asked.

The old woman ignored her. "When you find your cat, you won't be able to leave so easily. The giant has many evil friends."

She untied a string from a leather bag she wore around her waist and took out a kernel of corn. She gave it to Mattie. "Say, 'pop, corn, pop' when the time is right."

Mattie took the corn.

The old woman pushed back her hood, revealing scraggly white hair. She plucked a hair from her head and gave it to Sophie.

"When you need this, say, 'blow, hair, blow.'

Remember, each charm can only be used once. Choose wisely!"

"What about me?" Alex asked. "In stories, things always come in threes. Don't you have a charm for me?"

"I only had two charms left." The old woman covered her head again and pointed with one bony arm. "The path to the castle is that way."

Then the old woman began to shrink. Her cloak sprouted feathers and her worn shoes became talons. With a hateful hiss, she flapped her great wings and soared off.

Alex gawked. "That was the owl we saw earlier!"

Mattie wrinkled her nose at the kernel in her hand. "Do you think the charms are real?"

Alex shrugged. "What's real? We're in a fairy tale."

Sophie twisted the silver hair around her little finger.

"Back to the castle," Alex said to Sophie. "To get your dumb cat."

"Winchester is *not* dumb," said Sophie.

"Maybe not, but he isn't worth all this trouble," Mattie said. "When we catch him, he's going to the vet for a whole month!"

The kids found the path through the woods. They crossed the meadow and over the drawbridge. The double doors were still open.

A *trap*? Alex wondered.

They crept down the corridor, whispering Winchester's name and peeking into rooms.

"He could be anywhere," Mattie said. "This castle is huge."

Sophie said, "Shh! I hear little paws."

"Where?" Alex asked.

Sophie pointed. "There. He's walking on something soft."

They rushed to a room across the hall-way. Inside were a few chairs, a chest with drawers, and a four-poster bed the size of a boat. A blue rug like a fuzzy lake covered the slate floor. Winchester tiptoed across the rug, ignoring the kids in the doorway, then leaped lightly up on the bed. As he did, something tinkled. A patchwork quilt with squares of red and blue calico draped the bed. Stitched along its borders were hundreds of tiny silver bells. Winchester batted one of the bells with his paw. The bell tinkled, a sweet, delicate sound.

Alex noticed the giant's boots parked next to the bed and looked upward. Under the quilt, the giant himself made a whale-shaped lump. A white cloth was wrapped around his head.

"You were right about his headache," Alex whispered to Mattie.

Just then the giant's wife entered the room. She didn't see the kids hiding behind the cupboard.

"What are you doing in bed in the middle of the day?" she asked.

"THOSE PESKY KIDS," he replied. "THEY GAVE ME A HEADACHE."

"If you did a little work, you'd feel better," his wife said. "Why don't you take out the trash? Leg bones are clear up to the ceiling."

Alex swallowed. Leg bones? As in, *human* bones?

"LEAVE ME BE," the giant said, sneezing again. The cloth flew off his forehead. "I THINK I'M ALLERGIC TO SOMETHING."

"You're allergic to work." She left, mumbling,

"My mother told me to marry a doctor, but did I listen?"

Winchester sat near the giant's pillow. He lifted one hind leg and began licking. The giant lay with his eyes closed, unaware of the cat's presence.

Someone nudged Alex. It was Jackie. Her braids stuck out more wildly than ever. She grinned as brightly as the knife in her belt.

"What are you doing here?" he whispered. "We sent you home!"

"Thought I'd help you fetch your cat," she said. She nodded at Winchester nestled in the giant's pillow. "He leads a risky life, doesn't he?"

The giant sneezed again, setting the bells tinkling. "A LITTLE MUSIC. THAT'S WHAT I NEED," he said to himself. "PLAY."

Alex stiffened. The third treasure. In Sophie's story, the giant had a golden harp that sang. So far everything had been different in their story. Their ending would be different too. Would they live happily ever after?

The bells on the quilt began to chime the most beautiful music Alex had ever heard. At first the music was eerie. Then the bells rang a chorus so sad, he wanted to cry. Next the bells perked up and played a jaunty tune that had Jackie tapping her foot.

The giant had fallen asleep. Snores issued from his gaping mouth, causing the window shades to flap.

"I mean to have that bed-quilt," Jackie declared, over the giant's roof-raising snores.

"Are you crazy?" Mattie said. "What are you going to do? Ask the giant to hand it over?"

"You're good at thinkin' up plans," Jackie said to Alex. "I bet you can figure out a way to get the bed-quilt and the cat both."

Alex looked around at the boots and chairs. *Yes*, he thought. It *might work*.

He told the others.

Mattie shook her head. "We need to keep the giant busy. How about pepper?"

"Even better," Alex said.

"Soph and I will get the pepper shaker," Mattie said.

When they had gone, Alex and Jackie crept out from behind the cupboard. Together, they shoved the giant's boots under the bed. Then they tied the bootlaces in knots. Mattie and Sophie returned, dragging the pepper shaker between them.

"Now what?" said Jackie.

"Let's move these chairs," Alex answered.

It was slow work, but at last the four of them managed to heave two of the chairs against the bed, one on each side.

"Now comes the fun part."

Alex scaled the quilt near the giant's head, careful not to jingle the bells. When he was standing on the bedpost, he motioned for Jackie and Mattie to hand up the pepper shaker.

The giant's snores nearly knocked Alex off-balance. He steadied himself so he wouldn't tumble into the crater below. He waited until the giant's mouth was wide as a barn door.

Then Alex turned the pepper shaker over and hopped up and down. Pepper flakes fell into the giant's mouth in a black blizzard. He woke up, sucking in a big gulp of pepper-dusted air.

"HAAACKKK!" The giant bolted upright, coughing and choking. Tears streamed from his eyes and his nose dripped like a faucet. Then the sneezing began.

"A-A-A-CHOO! AA-CHOOO!" The giant squinted his watery eyes at Alex.

"YOU!" he wheezed, throwing back the jingling quilt.

Alex dropped the pepper shaker onto the giant's head and jumped down. He signaled the others to go into action. Sophie climbed up the other side of the bed, picked up Winchester, and slid down the quilt. Jackie and Mattie tugged one corner of the quilt, pulling it off the bed. Jackie wadded up the quilt and stuffed it under her arm like a football. They tore out of the room. Behind them, the giant leaped out of bed, bumping into the chairs.

"I'LL KILL THOSE KIDS!" he bellowed. "WIFE, WHERE ARE MY BOOTS!"

They heard him thrashing around the room, hunting for his boots. Alex figured they had a good head start. They pelted down the hall and over the drawbridge. The meadow was a blur of red and purple as they raced through it.

"I found a better way to the pea vine," Jackie said, as they struggled up the mountain. "It's faster." She switched the bundled quilt to the other arm.

"Help! Help!" cried a silvery voice. "Master, they're stealing me!"

"Make it be quiet!" Mattie said to Jackie. "The giant will know where we are!"

Jackie shook the quilt, which only made it shout louder.

"Help! Help!"

Alex threw a glance over his shoulder. "He's coming! Jackie, leave the quilt."

"No! I mean to give it to Mama."

They plunged into the forest. Jackie swerved to the right.

"This way," she said. The others followed in a ragged line.

"I think we're outrunning him," Alex said, noting that the crashing noises were fainter. "Maybe he's getting tired."

"So am I," Mattie complained. "I've never run so much in my life."

The woods had been calm and quiet, but now a strong wind ripped leaves off the trees. From out of nowhere, a flock of black-winged birds plummeted from the sky. Twenty or thirty crows dive-bombed the kids, cawing loudly. The biggest crow had coal black eyes glittering with hate. The leader aimed his wicked beak straight at Alex.

— 9 —

The Witch's Charms

Alex squeezed his eyes shut, expecting the stab of that pointy beak. Winchester tensed in his arms.

"Help!" the quilt screeched. "Master! Help!" The wind blew the bells, making a terrible racket.

"Mattie, use the corn!" Jackie yelled over the quilt's screeching.

Mattie reached into her pocket and drew out the grain of corn.

"Now!" Jackie shouted.

Throwing the corn at the crow leader, Mattie shouted, "Pop, corn, pop!"

The single kernel burst into bushels of fluffy white popcorn. The greedy crows attacked the popcorn, gorging themselves.

"The charm worked!" said Mattie.

"I told you," Jackie said. "The witch's charms always work."

Alex stared at her. "How did you know about the witch?"

Beneath their feet, the earth drummed with the giant's steady steps. *Thrum!* *Thrum!*

"FEE, FAW, FUMM!" the giant intoned.

"Make tracks!" Jackie said, and raced off.

Alex shifted Winchester and pushed Sophie ahead of him. He and Mattie dashed after Jackie.

They plunged into the forest. Spindly pines gave way to oak trees cloaked in honeysuckle and choking vines. The kids fought to get through.

Alex didn't remember fairy tales being so *long*. Whenever he read a story to Sophie, it only took a few minutes. He felt as if he'd been in this story for years.

A shower of leaves fell on his head. When Alex looked back, he saw the giant looming against the sky.

"YOU'LL BE IN MY STEWPOT TONIGHT!" he said gleefully.

Alex wasn't about to be in anybody's stewpot. He spurted ahead of Jackie. The trees grew sparser. Soon they could see the snowy cloud bank.

"Yay!" Mattie cheered.

Just then a freezing wind rammed into them, dotted with snowflakes. The snowflakes formed shapes. Long muzzles, pointed ears, blue eyes chipped from ice. Knife-blade teeth.

Wolves!

A pack of white wolves with snow-glistened fur lunged at the kids, fangs bared.

The wolves encircled the kids, snarling and growling. The largest wolf broke from the pack. His eyes were so pale that they were ghostly white. And they were fixed on Sophie.

Alex gripped Winchester, who clawed to escape.

"Sophie!" he shrieked, as the wolf charged.

— 10 —

Happily Ever After?

Sophie stood like she was carved from ice. The wolf was a hair away from her throat, its jaws snapping.

"Use the hair!" Alex shouted to break her trance. "Remember the words!"

Sophie raised her hand. The old woman's white hair shimmered around her little finger.

"Blow, hair, blow!" she yelled, letting go of the hair.

A stiff wind caught the hair and carried it upward. The wolf pack leader dropped mid-snap. The wolves disappeared in a puff of fog, and the clouds softened again.

"FEE, FAW, FUMM—"

The kids had forgotten about the giant. Now he stamped toward them, grinning fiendishly.

"IS THAT ANY WAY TO TREAT MY FRIENDS?"

"Lookee there!" Jackie said. "The pea vine!"

The curly tendrils and heart-shaped leaves of the pea vine rose above clouds.

"Nice knowin' you!" Jackie bounded across the clouds, leaving the others dazed.

"Why isn't she waiting for us?" Mattie asked.

"Never mind," Alex cried. "Run!"

"OH NO, YOU DON'T!"

Alex hoped the giant's trunklike legs would punch through the pillowy clouds. No such luck. The clouds dented under the giant's weight but sprang back like elastic.

Jackie stood by the pea vine. She tied the quilt around her waist, and then hopped down the vine without a backward glance. When the kids reached the vine a few minutes later, Mattie vaulted down the main trunk first.

"I thought you were afraid of heights," Alex said.

"I'm more afraid of *him*," she said, and lost no time finding a foothold.

Sophie went next, after tucking Ellsworth in her shirt.

"I can't carry you anymore," Alex said to Winchester. "You're on your own." Clearly tired of adventures, the cat scrabbled down the vine.

With a last glance at the giant, who was still wading through the clouds, Alex popped down the vine like a prairie dog in his hole. It was much easier going down than up. He grasped a thick, smooth trunk and shinnied down like he was sliding down a spiraling fire pole.

Down, down, down he went, every now and then catching a glimpse of Winchester's tail, of Sophie's head, of Ellsworth's red-velvet ears. He passed through the drifting, wispy clouds and emerged, feeling damp.

Below Alex saw the molehill-size Blue Ridge Mountains and the horseshoe bends of a river. They were almost home!

The pea vine quivered violently. Alex looked up. To his horror, he spied the wide, muddy sole of the giant's boots.

Just like in the story, he thought.

"He's after us!" Alex called down. "Don't stop!"

The vine quaked like a bucking bronco. Alex worried that the giant would shake them off. They had to reach the ground before the giant did.

The giant wasn't quite as nimble as the kids. They scrambled down like monkeys, hand over hand. The mountains grew from molehills into true mountains. Treetops came into view and then rooftops. Alex strained to spot the chimneys of the Gray Horse Inn. He was never so glad to see the old house in his life! He dropped the last few feet, landing in their backyard. Mattie, Sophie, and Winchester waited for him.

"Where's Jackie?" he asked.

Mattie pointed to the girl ripping through the garden.

"Stay here," Alex said, and took off after Jackie.

His legs hurt from all the climbing and running but he couldn't let her get away. Jackie must have been tired too, because he easily caught up with her and tackled her.

"Get up," he told her. "How did you know about the witch's charms?"

"The man-giant is coming!" she said, wide-eyed.

"I bet the old witch gave you the magic pea seeds," he pressed. "What did you trade besides your cow? It was *us*, wasn't it?"

Jackie hung her head. "The witch said she'd protect me from the man-giant, if I helped her capture you-all."

"But why?" Alex asked.

Jackie's freckled cheeks flushed. "The witch is feudin' with the man-giant. He scared off all the animals she ate when she was an owl. She needed kids. That's what the man-giant likes best."

"So she was going to give us to the giant?"

"Not all of you at once," Jackie said. "When the giant got good and hungry for flesh-meat, she was goin' to let one of you go."

"Then why did she help us escape?" Alex asked.

"After I told her how you'd helped me fight the man-giant, she decided it would be better to get rid of him," Jackie replied. "She gave you the charms so you'd lure him down the pea vine."

"Alex!" Mattie screamed. The vine shuddered as the giant climbed steadily downward.

"We helped you," Alex said to Jackie. "And this is the thanks we get."

"I'm sorry," Jackie said, and it sounded like she meant it. "I didn't figure you-all would be so nice."

Alex looked at her and nodded. "Okay. Things will be even if you help us now."

"Deal."

They ran back to the base of the vine where Mattie shielded Sophie. The giant's boots were almost directly overhead. He laughed when he saw the kids on the ground.

"There are really three charms," said Jackie. "The witch gave me one."

She drew the hunting knife from her waistband. Flashing the blade, she commanded, "Chop, knife, chop!"

The knife leaped out of her hand and began hacking at the vine. It cut through the thick twined branches like a buzz saw. The vine tilted with the giant hanging on.

"HEY!" he yelled in surprise.

The giant grabbed branches and leaves in a desperate attempt to stay upright. The base splintered with a deafening crack.

"Tim-ber!" Alex cried, as the enormous pea vine toppled to the ground.

The garden rippled in mighty, violent waves, as if someone were shaking a mammoth rug. The fur on Winchester's back stood up in a frightened ridge.

CRASH!

The kids stared. The vine lay like a gigantic snake all over the garden. A smothering heap of tendrils and leaves surrounded the birdbath and goldfish pond. The giant's bulbous nose and satellite-dish ears stuck up from a pile of leaves. His thatch of red hair grazed the bottom of the tower. His eyes were closed.

"Is he dead?" Sophie asked fearfully.

"Only one way to find out." Alex crept up to the giant, using the fallen vine as cover. His enormous chest swelled and fell slowly. "He's alive! But when he wakes up, he's going to be awful mad."

"Time for me to strike out for home," Jackie said.

"Where do you live, anyway?" asked Mattie.

Jackie pointed to Wildcat Mountain. "Our

cabin's in Possum Holler. I guess you are already home."

"Sort of," Alex said.

While their surroundings seemed familiar, the house and garden still wore a faded, old-timey look.

"Come on up and see Mama and me some-time," Jackie offered. "We'll pull up a stool and gnaw on a hambone."

Sophie crinkled her nose. "That doesn't sound like much fun."

Jackie laughed, and then sprinted across the garden, hurdling over the vine. The quilt jingled merrily.

When she was out of sight, Alex said, "Ready to go back?"

"Yes," said Mattie, "and hurry before Mom or Dad comes out. They won't like a giant in their garden."

"They won't ever see him. Remember? This isn't really home." Alex pulled the spyglass from his pocket and held it out by one end. "Soph, grab Winchester."

She hauled the big cat over her shoulder, and then grasped the middle of the spyglass. Mattie took the other end.

Alex's feet plummeted. For a second, he felt like he was falling down the pea vine. Bright lights flickered behind his eyelids. Red, blue, purple. Not so much green this time.

Thud.

His sneakers hit something solid: the floor of the tower room. When the others appeared beside him, they all rushed to the window. No great, green vine blocked the sun, which streamed warmly through the glass. No chopped-down vine on their garden. Best of all, no conked-out giant at the bottom of the tower.

They were truly home.

Winchester flopped down on Sophie's book of fairy tales and yawned.

"*Now* you want to rest," Mattie said to the cat, her hands on her hips.

"So do I," said Alex, collapsing next to the cat. "I wasn't this tired when we went on the dinosaur dig. Who ever said fairy tales were for sissies?"

"You did," Sophie said. "Lots of times."

"Well, I take it back."

Sophie opened the book, flipping the pages. "Here's Jackie."

Alex studied the illustration that showed a boy climbing a beanstalk. The boy was barefoot and wore old clothes. His brown hair stuck out in cowlicks, and freckles dusted his nose. The caption beneath read, "Jack climbs the beanstalk."

The boy's face was Jackie's.

"You're right, Soph," said Mattie. "Did anybody understand this trip? I don't."

"The postcard message was from the quilt," Alex figured. "It kept yelling, 'Help.' We didn't save it from Jackie, though."

"It has a better home," said Sophie. "Jackie and her mother won't make it play all the time like the giant did."

"I guess we completed our mission," Mattie said. "But we nearly got trapped."

"I think we learned that magic is unpredictable," said Alex. "And that you have to go by your feelings."

Mattie nodded. "We didn't use the charms accidentally. We were meant to pull out the right one at the right time."

"Because we were the good guys," said Sophie.

"Was this trip fun for you?" Alex asked her.

She hugged Ellsworth, grinning. "Yeah! I like going into stories!"

"Well, I hope we go on a normal adventure next time. Fairy tales are scary!" Alex put the spyglass back in the desk. Then he opened the bottom drawer and took out an envelope.

"The Travel Guide's letter will tell us more," Mattie said.

Alex closed the drawer and headed for the bookcase panel. "Let's go downstairs to read it."

While he pivoted the bookcase, Mattie scooped up Winchester.

"Let's go, buster," she said, burying her face in his fur.

Sophie lagged behind, sliding open one of the cubbyholes in the desk.

"Soph, we're leaving," Alex said. What was she doing?

"Coming!" She dropped something inside.

Before she slid the drawer closed again, Alex thought he heard the silvery jingle of a bell. No, he must be imagining things.

Dear Mattie, Alex, and Sophie:

This trip was certainly different! What did you think? I know Alex doesn't believe fairy tales are for sissies any more!

You're probably wondering why you went to an imaginary land instead of some place "real." Sophie will tell you that made-up stories are just as important as real-life stories.

Humans have always told stories. Some stories helped people learn about who they were. Some were just for fun. Stories passed from one generation to the next. Later, men began visiting villages and towns. Their mission was to keep old stories from being forgotten. They listened to the old tales and wrote them down.

Joseph Jacobs, who lived from 1854 to 1916, sat by many fireplaces in England, listening to people tell stories. He copied down tales, such as "The

Three Bears" and "Jack and the Beanstalk"

Jacobs first heard "Jack in the Beanstalk" when he was a child in Australia around 1860. English people settled in Australia in the early 1800s. When Jacobs heard his childhood tale told in England, he realized that stories traveled like suitcases. He published "Jack and the Beanstalk," and many other stories, in a book called English Fairy Tales, in 1890.

People who came to America brought their stories with them. The colonists, who settled in the mountain regions of Virginia, Georgia, North Carolina, Tennessee, Kentucky, and West Virginia, told the most colorful tales. Tales were even swapped on Wildcat Mountain, in your backyard! But a funny thing happened—the longer the colonists lived in the mountains, the more the stories changed. "Jack and the Beanstalk" became "Jack and the Bean Tree" or "Jack and the Wonder Beans."

How do we know this? In 1935, a farmer in Beech Creek, North Carolina, told historian Richard Chase "Jack and the Bean Tree." He also told other stories about Jack. In Jacobs's book, the giant says, "Fee-fi-fo-fum, I smell the blood of an Englishman. Be he alive or be he dead, I'll grind his bones to eat with my bread." The giant's speech changed with the way the mountain people spoke. In their stories, the giant says, "Fee-faw-fumm, I smell the blood of an English-mum. Bein' he dead or bein' he alive, I'll grind his bones to eat with my pones." (Pone is a type of cornbread.)

I hope that you enjoyed this trip into an "old handed-down tale." Remember, the first definition of history is "story." Next time, you will go back in time to a real place of magic. But you didn't hear this from me!

Yours in time,
"Mr. Taylor"

TIME SPIES MISSION NO. 3
GROW A SPY GARDEN

On this trip, you learned that plants—even Wonder Pea seeds—are handed down like stories. You can find out a lot about a place from the plants that grow in the soil. You learned that the strange plant in your garden, twinleaf, came from Thomas Jefferson's garden. Jefferson traded seeds with farmers, plantation owners, and probably the very first family that lived at the Gray Horse Inn.

Until your next Time Spies adventure, your mission is to investigate your own backyard. What can you find out by growing your own spy garden of mystery plants?

WHAT YOU NEED:

An old, fuzzy sock
Shoebox
Potting soil
Scissors
Plastic wrap

WHAT YOU DO:

1. Slip the sock over your shoe. Now take a hike! With your parent or a friend, go outside and walk around your yard, a field, the park, anywhere plants are growing. Take giant-size steps. Cover as much ground as you can.

2. Line the shoebox with plastic wrap. Fill it with potting soil.

3. Cut your sock so you can lay it flat. Notice the seeds stuck to it Put the sock in the shoebox with the seeds pointing up. Cover with more soil and water.

4. Check your spy garden in a week. The seeds should have sprouted.
5. Let the sprouts grow into seedlings. Be sure to keep watering.
6. Look in a local field guide or take your spy garden to a nursery and ask for help in identifying your mystery plants!

TIME SPIES

"A time-traveling mystery . . . that will keep kids turning the pages!"
—Marcia T. Jones,
co-author of *The Bailey School Kids*

Give an important message to General Washington in
Secret in the Tower

MIRRORS... ...U.S.A.